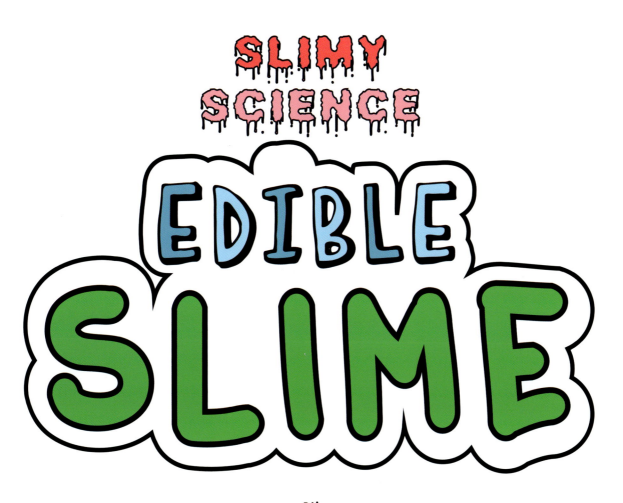

SLIMY SCIENCE
EDIBLE SLIME

BY
LOUISE NELSON

Published in 2022 by Windmill Books,
an Imprint of Rosen Publishing
29 East 21st Street, New York, NY 10010

© 2022 Booklife Publishing
This edition is published by arrangement with Booklife Publishing

All rights reserved. No part of this book may be reproduced in any form without permission in writing from the publisher, except by a reviewer.

Edited by: Madeline Tyler
Illustrated by: Danielle Rippengill

Cataloging-in-Publication Data

Names: Nelson, Louise.
Title: Edible slime / Louise Nelson.
Description: New York : Windmill, 2022. | Series: Slimy science | Includes glossary and index.
Identifiers: ISBN 9781499489538 (pbk.) | ISBN 9781499489552 (library bound) | ISBN 9781499489545 (6pack) | ISBN 9781499489569 (ebook)
Subjects: LCSH: Gums and resins, Synthetic--Juvenile literature. | Handicraft--Juvenile literature.
Classification: LCC TP978.N45 2022 | DDC 620.1'924--dc23

Printed in the United States of America

CPSIA Compliance Information: Batch CWWM22: For Further Information contact Rosen Publishing, New York, New York at 1-800-237-9932

SAFETY AND RESPONSIBILITY INFO FOR GROWN-UPS

Any ingredients used could cause irritation, so don't play with slime for too long, don't put it near your face, and keep it away from babies and young children.

Always wash your hands before and after making slime. Choose kid-safe glues and non-toxic ingredients, and always make sure there is an adult present.

Don't substitute ingredients—we cannot guarantee the results.

Leftover slime can be stored for one more use for up to a week in a sealed container and out of the reach of children. For hygiene reasons, we do not recommend storing slime that has been used in a classroom environment.

Slime is not safe for pets.

Wear a mask around powdered ingredients and goggles around liquid ingredients. Before throwing your slime away, cut it into lots of small pieces. Don't put slime down the drain—always put it in the trash.

MARSHMALLOW SLIME!

IMAGE CREDITS: All images are courtesy of Shutterstock.com, unless otherwise specified. With thanks to Getty Images, Thinkstock Photo and iStockphoto. Cover – Zhe Vasylieva, balabolka, Dado Photos, xnova, Lithiumphoto, KAMONWAN SIRIWAN, KlavdiyaV, Lena Havryliuk. Images used on every page: Heading Font – Zhe Vasylieva. Background – Lithiumphoto. Grid – xnova. Splats – Sonechko57. 2 – Hong Vo. 4 – Dado Photos. 5 – Hong Vo, Dado Photos, Stenko Vlad. 6 – Henri Koskinen. 7 – New Africa. 8 – SmLyubov, VLADIMIR VK, VLADIMIR VK. 10 – Pises Tungittipokai, Tsyb Oleh, Pressmaster. 11 – jarabee123, KAMONWAN SIRIWAN, Nadya Buyanowa. 12 – Natali Zakharova. 13 – all_about_people, Elena Blokhina, GOLFX, Jennie Book. 14 – Hong Vo, Dado Photos, Stenko Vlad Tom Van Dyck. 16 – all_about_people. 17 – New Africa, Nishihama, Firn. 18 – Nacho Mena. 19 – Artiom Photo, Dado Photos, Fleckstone, Ory Gonian. 20 – jarabee123, Volodymyr Plysiuk, Keizerphoto33. 22 – Sergiy Kuzmin. 23 – KAMONWAN SIRIWAN.

CONTENTS

PAGE 4	IT'S SLIME TIME!
PAGE 6	THE SCIENCE OF SLIME
PAGE 8	ASKING QUESTIONS
PAGE 9	SAFETY FIRST!
PAGE 10	THE SENSES
PAGE 12	MARSHMALLOW PUTTY
PAGE 14	FOR SCIENCE!
PAGE 16	CHIA SEED SLIME
PAGE 18	GUMMY SLIME
PAGE 20	LET'S EXPERIMENT
PAGE 24	GLOSSARY AND INDEX

Words that look like this can be found in the glossary on page 24.

IT'S SLIME TIME!

It's sticky. It's oozy. It stretches and bounces. It's slime! Slime is . . . well . . . it's like . . . It's certainly hard to explain! What is slime, really?

!! NERD ALERT !!
Slime is a non-Newtonian fluid. This means that it doesn't act like other liquids, such as water or milk.

Everything you can see around you is made of something, right? What are your shoes made of? Or the walls around you? How about a spoon or a car? The things these items are made of are called materials.

SLIME IS A MATERIAL THAT HAS THE FOLLOWING PROPERTIES:

NOT QUITE SOLID

SQUEEZY

FLOWS BUT ISN'T RUNNY

STRETCHY

NOT QUITE LIQUID

THE SCIENCE OF SLIME

Living slime might sound like a nightmare, but it's real! Slime mold looks like slime, but it can move and change shape!

TUBE SLIME MOLD

WE CAN ALSO MAKE SLIME WITH FOOD!

Always make slime with an adult!

When we mix two **chemicals** together, it can change their properties. By mixing the correct ingredients together, we can turn everyday food ingredients into slime!

ASKING QUESTIONS

Asking questions can help scientists _investigate_ things. What questions can we ask about edible slime?

!! NERD ALERT !!
Most slime you buy or make is not safe to eat! DON'T EAT IT! Don't put any slime in your mouth unless you have checked with a grown-up first!

HOW FAR WILL IT STRETCH?

HOW STICKY IS IT?

HOW FAR DOES IT DRIP?

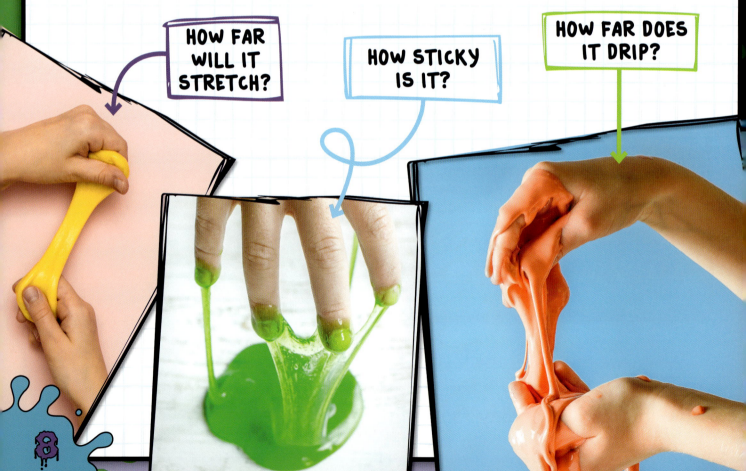

SAFETY FIRST!

THE GOLDEN RULES

1. Always make slime with a grown-up.

2. These recipes are edible, but do not eat or swallow any other types of slime.

3. Always check with an adult before eating the slimes in this book.

!! NERD ALERT !!

If you are <u>sensitive</u> to any ingredients, wear long sleeves and gloves or use a different recipe.

THE SENSES

WE CAN EXPLORE TASTE-SAFE SLIMES WITH ALL FIVE SENSES:

Our five main senses tell us about the world around us.

We can **TOUCH** it with our hands.

We can **SEE** what colors it is.

!! **NERD ALERT** !!
Remember, only taste slime which has been made with all food ingredients. Always check with a grown-up first.

We can **SMELL** and sniff it.

We can **HEAR** it squelch.

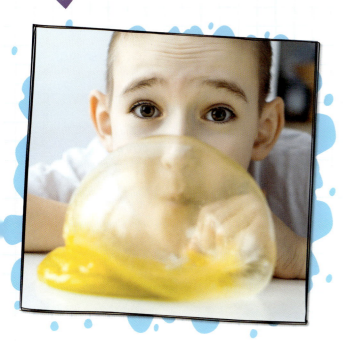

We can **TASTE** its flavors.

MARSHMALLOW PUTTY

TO MAKE MARSHMALLOW PUTTY, YOU WILL NEED:

- ☐ Marshmallows
- ☐ 1 tablespoon of cooking oil
- ☐ Half a tablespoon of cornstarch
- ☐ Microwave-safe bowl
- ☐ Microwave
- ☐ Spoon

DON'T FORGET!
Always make slime with a responsible adult and wash your hands before touching food.

(and extra for dusting)

Melted marshmallows are HOT, so be careful.

Always let an adult use the microwave and test the marshmallows.

METHOD:

1. Put a handful of marshmallows in a bowl, and add the cooking oil.

2. Microwave until they are soft and like liquid (30-40 seconds).

3. Wait one minute, then add the cornstarch and carefully mix.

4. When the mixture is cool enough to touch, dust your table with cornstarch and **knead** the slime until it feels like putty.

13

FOR SCIENCE!

Let's make some *observations* about your creations! Explore your marshmallow slime with all five senses...

Write down what you notice about your slime in a notebook.

SENSE	OBSERVATION
Touch	Soft, smooth
Smell	Sweet
Taste	Sweet—and floury!
Sight	Pink, matte
Sound	Squelches when squeezed!

!! NERD ALERT !!
Remember, do not eat all your slime,
just a small taste is enough!

CHIA SEED SLIME

TO MAKE CHIA SEED SLIME, YOU WILL NEED:

- [ ] 1/4 cup (50 g) of chia seeds
- [ ] 1 3/4 cups (about 400 ml) of water
- [ ] A few drops of food coloring
- [ ] Cornstarch

DON'T FORGET! Always make slime with a responsible adult!

!! NERD ALERT !! Chia seeds need to soak for a few hours to get slimy, so plan ahead!

METHOD:

1. Add the chia seeds, water, and food coloring to a container.

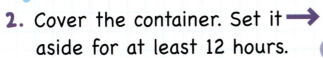

2. Cover the container. Set it aside for at least 12 hours.

3. Your chia seed mixture will turn into a slimy liquid!

4. Stir in the cornstarch a spoonful at a time. When it gets too hard to stir, knead instead.

5. Add cornstarch until you get the <u>texture</u> you want.

GUMMY SLIME

TO MAKE THIS SWEET SLIME, YOU WILL NEED:

- ☐ 2 handfuls of gummy candy
- ☐ 1 tablespoon of powdered sugar
- ☐ 1 tablespoon of cornstarch
- ☐ Microwave-safe bowl
- ☐ Spoon

!! NERD ALERT !!
Separate your gummies by color for a bright slime, or mix to make new colors!

(and a bit more just in case)

Melted gummies are HOT! Let an adult melt and stir until the mixture is cool.

METHOD:

1. Heat the gummies in the microwave until they are melted.

2. Stir until smooth.

3. Add the cornstarch and powdered sugar to the gummies, and mix.

4. When the mixture is cool, knead in more cornstarch and powdered sugar until it is the texture you want.

LET'S EXPERIMENT

Now that you have made several types of slime, we can compare them. This means we will play with each slime and notice how they are the same and how they are different.

HOW MANY WORDS CAN YOU THINK OF TO DESCRIBE EACH SLIME? DON'T FORGET TO USE ALL FIVE SENSES!

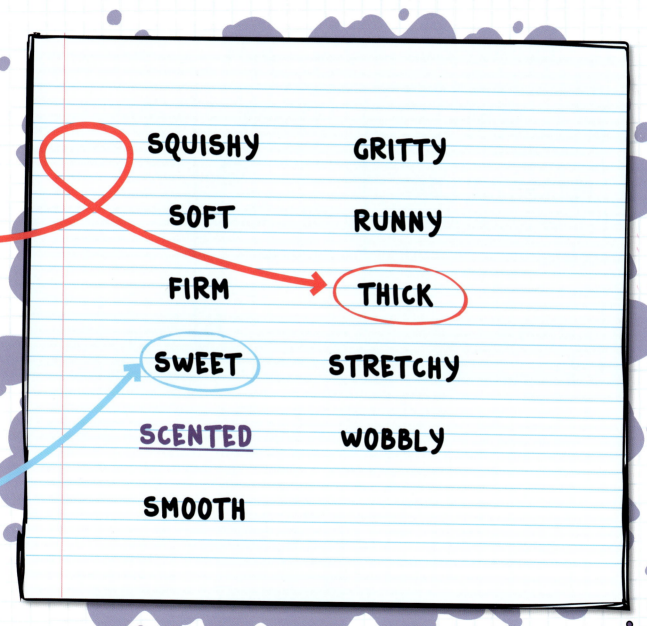

SQUISHY   GRITTY

SOFT   RUNNY

FIRM   THICK

SWEET   STRETCHY

SCENTED   WOBBLY

SMOOTH

LET'S RECORD ALL OF OUR FINDINGS IN A TABLE LIKE THIS.

FINDINGS:

SLIME	TOUCH	TASTE
MARSHMALLOW		
CHIA	Gritty	
GUMMY		Sweet

Here are a few more ideas for making tasty slime. Can you test these and record your findings too?

Use green gummies to make edible snot! Ew!

WHAT OTHER WORDS CAN YOU COME UP WITH?

SMELL	LOOK	SOUNDS
Yummy!		

Use cocoa powder and white marshmallows to make chocolate slime. It smells amazing!

Add popcorn for crunchy texture!

GLOSSARY

CHEMICALS — matter that can cause changes to other matter when mixed

INVESTIGATE — look closely and carefully at something to find an answer

KNEAD — mix something by pressing, pulling, and folding

LIQUIDS — materials that flow, such as water

MATTE — not shiny

OBSERVATIONS — things found out from watching something carefully

PROPERTIES — features of something

SCENTED — giving off a smell

SENSITIVE — reacts strongly to something

SOLID — firm and stable, not a liquid

TEXTURE — the feel of something

INDEX

CHEMICALS 7
CHIA SEEDS 16–17, 20, 22
GUMMIES 18–20, 22
MARSHMALLOWS 12–14, 20, 22–23
OBSERVATIONS 14–15, 20–23
PROPERTIES 5, 7
SENSES 10–11, 14–15, 21
SOLIDS 5
STRETCHING 4, 5, 8, 21